Little Red Riding Hood

Retold and Illustrated by
Fred Crump, Jr.

TO SOW THE FALLOW SOIL

Winston-Derek Publishers, Inc.
Pennywell Drive—P.O. Box 90883
Nashville, TN 37209

1

First printing

PUBLISHED BY WINSTON-DEREK PUBLISHERS, INC.
Nashville, Tennessee 37205

Library of Congress Catalog Card No: 88-50758
ISBN: 1-55523-193-4

Printed in the United States of America

Little Red Riding Hood

Retold and Illustrated by
Fred Crump, Jr.

Once, not too long ago and not too far away, there lived a little girl named Sarah Jane Jimson.

For her seventh birthday her granny made her a red velvet cape with a hood. And from that day on, Sarah Jane was called Little Red Riding Hood.

One day Little Red Riding Hood's mother asked her to take a basket of goodies to Granny.

ow, Granny lived in another part of the forest, a long walk away. So Little Red Riding Hood's mother cautioned her:

"Don't dawdle along the way.
Don't stray off the path.
And don't talk to strangers."

"Yes, Ma'am," she said, and went skipping off into the woods.

It happened to be a beautiful spring day. There were bright butterflies to chase and bunnies to watch and birds to sing with and tortoises to tickle and . . .

. . . Little Red Riding Hood dawdled along the way.

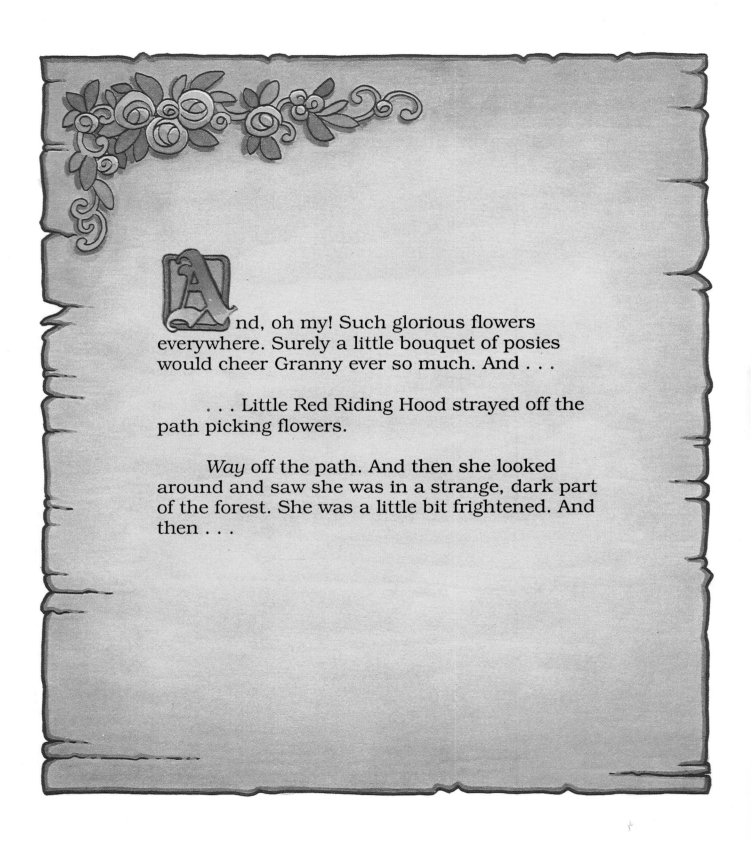

And, oh my! Such glorious flowers everywhere. Surely a little bouquet of posies would cheer Granny ever so much. And . . .

. . . Little Red Riding Hood strayed off the path picking flowers.

Way off the path. And then she looked around and saw she was in a strange, dark part of the forest. She was a little bit frightened. And then . . .

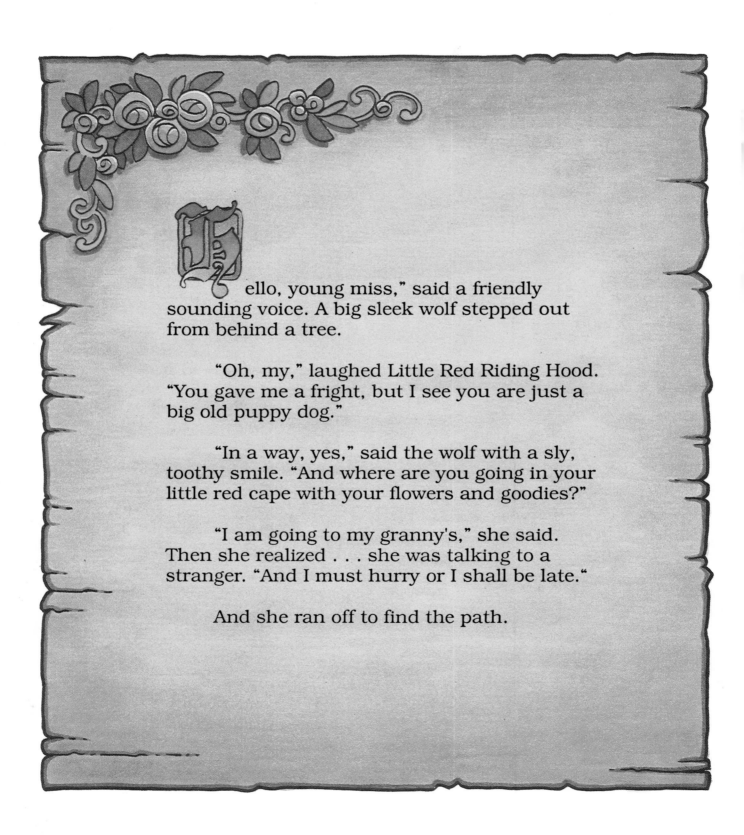

ello, young miss," said a friendly sounding voice. A big sleek wolf stepped out from behind a tree.

"Oh, my," laughed Little Red Riding Hood. "You gave me a fright, but I see you are just a big old puppy dog."

"In a way, yes," said the wolf with a sly, toothy smile. "And where are you going in your little red cape with your flowers and goodies?"

"I am going to my granny's," she said. Then she realized . . . she was talking to a stranger. "And I must hurry or I shall be late."

And she ran off to find the path.

erhaps we shall meet again," called the wolf. And then with a growly chuckle, he added, "Soon!"

Well, it seems this sly old wolf knew all parts of the forest. And he knew where Granny's cottage was, so he took a quick shortcut through the woods, and . . .

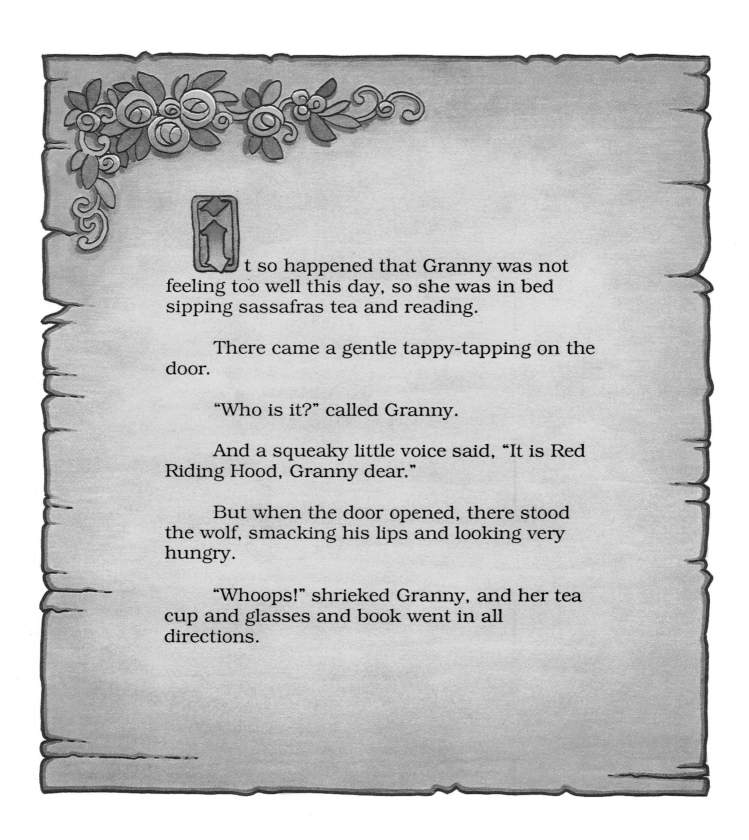

It so happened that Granny was not feeling too well this day, so she was in bed sipping sassafras tea and reading.

There came a gentle tappy-tapping on the door.

"Who is it?" called Granny.

And a squeaky little voice said, "It is Red Riding Hood, Granny dear."

But when the door opened, there stood the wolf, smacking his lips and looking very hungry.

"Whoops!" shrieked Granny, and her tea cup and glasses and book went in all directions.

he wolf leaped at the bed and made a big gulping "Chomp!" But by then Granny was out the back door and all the wolf got was a mouth full of feather pillow.

ever mind," grumped the wolf. "It is time for Red Riding Hood. I will be Granny," he said. Then he put on her lace cap and night dress and spectacles.

There came a knock at the door.

Just in time the wicked wolf jumped under the covers and called in a quavery granny voice, "Come in, my dear."

And Little Red Riding Hood came in with her little bouquet and basket of goodies. But she stopped.

"Why, Granny dear," she said, "you do not look yourself at all."

"I've been ill, my child," croaked the wolf.

"And how big your ears look," she said.

"The better to hear you with, my dearie dear," said the wolf.

"And your eyes are like saucers."

"The better to see you with, my little sunshine," cackled the wolf.

"And Granny, said Red Riding Hood, "how very big your teeth look today."

"All the better to EAT you with, my little dumpling!" laughed the wolf. Then he leaped out of bed and grabbed Little Red Riding Hood.

But just in time the door flew open with a crash. Granny had found the woodcutter. He rushed in shouting and swinging his axe.

"Uh oh!" whimpered the wolf when he saw the axe, and he let go of Red Riding Hood.

hen he gave a frightened yowl and ran out the door in a panic, with the woodcutter right at his heels.

The cowardly wolf ran so far and so fast that he finally got away. But he was never ever seen in the forest again.

hen Granny and the woodcutter and Red Riding Hood had a tea party with the basket of goodies. There were crispy cucumber sandwiches and juicy cherry tarts, and Granny made hot cinnamon tea.

And they laughed and laughed at the sight of the wolf in Granny's clothes.

Little Red Riding Hood thanked the woodcutter for saving her. And she kissed her granny on the nose and wished her good health. Then she said goodbye and started back home.

But this time . . .

She didn't dawdle.
She didn't stray from the path.
And she didn't speak to any strangers.